OSCAR

AND THE DOGNAPPERS

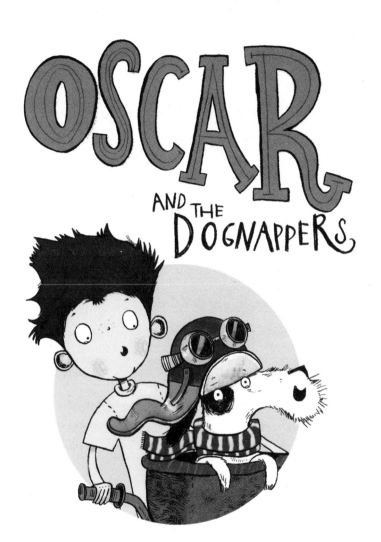

ALAN MACDONALD

ILLUSTRATED BY SARAH HORNE

EGMONT

**To our good friends Deb and Tim
and all the Martins.
AM**

**For our dogs, Millie and Sandy.
SH**

EGMONT
We bring stories to life

First published in Great Britain 2018
by Egmont UK Limited
The Yellow Building, 1 Nicholas Road, London W11 4AN

Text copyright © 2018 Alan MacDonald
Illustrations copyright © 2018 Sarah Horne

The moral rights of the author and illustrators have been asserted

ISBN 978 1 4052 8723 4

67271/1

A CIP catalogue record for this title is available from the British Library

Typeset by Avon DataSet Ltd, Bidford on Avon, Warwickshire
Printed and bound in Great Britain by the CPI Group

CONTENTS

Chapter 1

Smoke Signals

It was Saturday morning in the Shilling house and a delicious smell was drifting upstairs from the kitchen. Sam was in his room getting dressed. Downstairs his dad was cooking sausages. His mum sat at the kitchen table while Oscar sat on the floor because dogs generally didn't bother with chairs. Sausages, however, were his number-one favourite and his tail was beating the floor impatiently while he waited for them to cook. Dad slotted four pieces of bread into the Hercules Speedy Pop-up Toaster (one of his many inventions) and went back to turning the sausages.

'Have you noticed you can't get a decent cup of coffee round here?' he said.

'Mmm?' said Mum.

'Or tea or hot chocolate for that matter,' Dad went on. 'There's nowhere to buy it – not without walking all the way into town.'

'There's a drinks machine at the garage,' Mum pointed out.

Dad snorted. 'Have you actually tried their coffee?' he asked. 'I wouldn't give it to a dog!'

Oscar looked up and frowned. He sniffed the air and his tail ceased drumming for a moment. The Hercules Speedy Pop-up Toaster was taking its own sweet time. Stranger still, it was giving off a funny smell – a bit like burning toast. Oscar barked to get everyone's attention.

'Quiet, Oscar!' cried Mr Shilling. 'There's

nowhere on the seafront at all,' he said, returning to his subject. 'Don't you think that's odd?'

Oscar stared. Smoke was now rising from the toaster. It seemed impossible to miss, though everyone else was missing it. He decided he'd have to do something before things got out of hand. Trotting over to Mr Shilling he jumped up and pawed at the back of his legs.

'OSCAR!' cried Dad, turning round. 'What's the matter with him today?'

'He's probably hungry,' replied Mum. 'He can smell sausages.'

Oscar felt like howling. *The toaster!* he wanted to shout. *For dog's sake – LOOK!*

Mum poured milk into her cereal bowl.

'What's that funny smell?' she frowned. 'Can you smell it?'

Finally thought Oscar. He looked at Mrs Shilling then back at the toaster. No response. This was getting ridiculous. He lay down on the floor with his paws over his head as if preparing for an explosion.

Dad stared at him. 'Is he sick or something?'

Sam walked into the kitchen, still pulling on his sweatshirt.

Oscar sat up and barked loudly.

'What's up, Oscar?' asked Sam.

Oscar turned and looked back at the toaster and raised a paw to point.

'Something's burning!' cried Sam.

BEEP! BEEP! BEEP! BEEP!

Suddenly the smoke alarm in the kitchen went off making them all jump. Seconds later there was a deafening BANG! as the Hercules Speedy Pop-up Toaster burst into flames.

'THE TOASTER!' cried Dad, waving the frying pan as sausages cartwheeled onto the floor. Everyone started shouting at once.

'DO SOMETHING!'

'CALL 999!'

'PUT IT OUT, PUT IT OUT!'

It was Mum who actually did something, grabbing a towel to beat out the flames. Two charred pieces of bread popped up from the toaster with a clunk and promptly disintegrated.

There was a silence broken only by the sound of chomping and slobbering. Oscar felt it would be a great pity to let sausages go to waste, so he was eating them off the floor. Mum went over and opened a window to let out the smoke, before collapsing onto a chair.

'That toaster has got to go. Why can't we have a normal one?' she sighed.

'It must have overheated,' said Dad. 'It's easily fixed.'

Sam shook his head. 'Well it's a good job Oscar was paying attention,' he said.

'Oscar?' said Dad.

'Yes, I could hear him barking from upstairs,' said Sam. 'He was obviously trying to warn you!'

Dad blinked. 'He *was* barking, come to think of it,' he said. 'I told him to shut up.'

Mum bent down to pat Oscar on the head.

'Clever boy, Oscar, well done!' she said.

Oscar swallowed the last piece of sausage, which was hanging out of his mouth.

Oscar *was* clever, of course, though Sam knew his parents had no idea how clever. Ever since Oscar had arrived a few months ago on the number 9 bus, Sam had the feeling that the dog had adopted them. It was Oscar who had helped Mr Shilling sell his new invention, the Poopomatic, to the Town Council. These days a small fleet of Poopomatics patrolled the streets of Little Bunting keeping them clean and free from dog mess. This was the first time Mr Shilling had ever actually sold one of his inventions and Sam had been wondering what he planned to

do with all the money. He poured himself a bowl of Puffo Pops since Oscar had wolfed all the sausages.

'What was I saying before the toaster exploded?' asked Dad. 'Oh yes. A decent cup of coffee, that's what this town needs.'

'I'd rather have an adventure playground,' said Sam.

'Anyway, why do you keep going on about coffee?' asked Mum.

Mr Shilling smiled with the air of someone about to make an important announcement.

'Because,' he said, 'I've just bought a little cafe on the seafront.'

'WHAT?' Mum almost fell off her seat. 'You're not serious?'

'It's perfect,' said Dad. 'It's an old beach hut in a great spot down on the front. I thought it could be a summer season thing while I work on my inventions in the winter.'

Sam could hardly believe his ears.

'We're going to run a cafe?' he asked.

'It's news to me,' said Mum.

'I'll take you to see it,' promised Dad. 'Honestly, I think this could be the best idea I've ever had.'

Sam smiled. His dad had said exactly the same thing about the Grandem – a four-saddle bike for all the family, which had failed to sell a single model. A cafe was different though, thought Sam, you wouldn't fall off it while going round corners. Cafes served pizza, ice cream and chocolate brownies – which luckily were all things that he loved!

'Are you telling me you've spent *all* of our savings on some old beach hut?' demanded Mum.

'Of course not all,' said Dad. 'I had to keep some back because the place needs a bit of work.'

'And who's going to run this cafe and cook all the meals?' demanded Mum.

'Well *me*, obviously,' replied Dad.

'Crumble!' muttered Oscar to himself.

Dad looked round at Sam. 'What did you say?'

'Er . . . good idea,' answered Sam, shooting Oscar a warning look. He was right about one thing though: no one could claim that Dad was famous for his cooking. His speciality was beans on toast – and even then the toast was usually burnt.

Chapter 2

Dream Cafe

Sam stood outside the house waiting for Dad with Oscar. Dad was eager to take them to see the new cafe for themselves. Mum said she had too much to do this morning and would go another time.

'So what do you think?' Sam asked.

Oscar took his time, scratching himself. 'I've never seen the point of cafes,' he said.

You might have expected Sam to gasp or fall over backwards in amazement but by now he was used to the fact that Oscar could talk. It was a secret between the two of them. Oscar said that things would only get complicated if Sam's parents ever knew and it would cause an almighty fuss. Sam hadn't even told his best friend Louie, although keeping the secret wasn't always easy. Oscar said it was best to pretend that he was just an ordinary dog who happened to be very clever.

'A cafe's somewhere people go to eat and drink,' explained Sam.

'You can do that at home,' Oscar pointed out.

'Yes, I know, but people like eating out sometimes,' said Sam. 'It's kind of a treat.'

'Like biscuits you mean?' asked Oscar.

'Sort of. I expect you'll see when we get there,' said Sam.

It was hard to explain cafes to a dog and besides Dad was coming out of the house, so they had to stop talking.

They walked along the seafront for about a quarter of a mile, until Dad stopped and pointed. 'There it is,' he said, proudly.

Sam stared. He'd expected something with large windows, comfy booths and warm lighting – a cafe in other words – but this place resembled a rundown Scout hut. The outside needed painting, the windows were broken and the roof sagged as if an elephant had recently sat on it.

'You bought *that?*' said Sam.

Dad nodded. 'Of course, it needs a little work but you have to use a bit of imagination.'

Sam thought you'd need a whole lot of imagination.

Inside the hut there was a small puddle on the floor where the rain had got in. The

floorboards were pebble-dashed with seagull droppings.

Oscar padded around, sniffing in all the corners. The hut had two rooms and in the back one they found a tall cupboard, a rusty cooker and a sink, which all looked like they had been there since Roman times.

Sam wrinkled his nose. 'It's a bit stinky,' he complained.

'I know, but we can clean it up. With the counter over here, a lick of paint and better lighting it'll be the best cafe on the seafront,' argued Dad.

'The *only* cafe on the seafront,' said Sam.

'Exactly, which is why it can't possibly fail,' said Dad. 'It's just what this town needs. I don't know why I've never thought of it before.'

'I thought you wanted to make things –

inventions,' said Sam.

'I'll do that too, but this is kind of a reinvention,' explained Dad. 'I'm turning a neglected beach hut into a successful cafe.'

'Right, so what are you going to call it?' asked Sam.

'I haven't really thought. The Old Beach Cafe, I guess,' replied Dad.

Sam wrinkled his nose. 'Sounds a bit boring.'

'Or maybe the Seaview Cafe?'

'*Deathly* boring,' said Sam. 'What about *Oscar's*?'

Dad snorted. 'You can't have a cafe named after a dog!'

Oscar looked offended. In his opinion a lot of things could be named after dogs. Why have Henry Road when you could have Barkley Square or Oscar Avenue?

'What about the food?' Sam asked.

'Ah that's the really clever part,' said Dad. 'We won't serve all the usual stuff like burgers, chips or ice cream.'

'We won't?' said Sam.

'No, my idea is beautifully simple,' said Dad. 'We're going to serve TOAST.'

'Toast?' repeated Sam.

'Well obviously not *just* toast,' said Dad. 'Cheese on toast, beans on toast, egg on toast – in fact pretty much anything on toast!'

Sam frowned. 'But what if people don't *like* toast?' he asked.

'Everyone likes toast!' laughed Dad. 'And the great thing is it's simple, you can't go wrong with making toast.'

'You can if you burn it,' said Sam.

He suspected that toast was the one thing his

dad knew how to cook. Other dishes, like chilli con carne or lemon meringue pie for instance, he hadn't the faintest clue. Still, the cafe would certainly be different.

'So it's really a toast cafe?' he said.

'I suppose it is,' said Dad. 'In fact that's brilliant, Sam! The Toast Cafe – that's what we'll call it!'

'Oh my great-grandmothers!'

A familiar voice interrupted them. It was Mr Trusscot, their busybody neighbour and Leader of the Town Council, whose bald head was poking round the door. Oscar gave a low growl. He'd come to regard Trusscot as a mortal enemy ever since he'd tried to turn large parts of town into 'dog-free zones'.

Trusscot walked in and looked around, shaking his head.

'I heard a rumour that some idiot had bought this dump,' he said.

'As it happens you're looking at the idiot,' replied Dad.

'YOU?' Trusscot stared. 'What on earth for?'

'If you must know, it's going to be a beach cafe,' Sam informed him.

Trusscot bent over. He shook, making strange squeaky noises like a rusty gate. Sam realised he was laughing.

'A cafe? Oh hee hee hee! That's a good one!' he chortled.

'It's not a joke,' scowled Dad.

Mr Trusscot took out a hanky and wiped his eyes.

'Of course not, I mean just look at this place, it's got everything,' he said. 'Broken windows, a leaking roof and bird wotsit on the floor!'

'Very funny,' said Dad. 'You won't be laughing when this place is a roaring success.'

'A success? It'll never happen,' scoffed Mr Trusscot.

'I bet you it will,' replied Dad.

'Not a chance,' said Trusscot.

'Is that right?'

'Yes it is right, *actually!*'

Sam rolled his eyes. He'd heard better arguments than this in the school playground. Mr Trusscot produced his wallet and pulled out a note.

'Twenty pounds says that you'll never last a week,' he said.

'Twenty? Pah! Make it fifty,' said Dad.

'If you're so sure, why not a hundred?' replied Trusscot.

Sam looked alarmed. This was getting out

of hand. Mum would go up the wall if she found out Dad had bet Mr Trusscot a hundred pounds!

'If you're going to bet, at least make it interesting,' he said.

'How do you mean "interesting"?' asked Trusscot.

'Well it's a cafe, so why don't you make the bet about food?' asked Sam.

'Oh I see, you mean the loser has to eat a plate of snails or something,' said Trusscot.

'Or a seaweed sandwich,' said Dad.

Sam's eye fell on Oscar. 'How about a bowl of dog food?' he suggested.

Mr Trusscot turned pale. He couldn't stand dogs and just the smell of the gloopy, ghastly food they ate made him feel sick. There was no way he was ever going to eat it. Then again, he wouldn't have to, because he'd make sure he won.

'All right, you're on,' he said.

'Fine by me,' replied Dad.

'One week from the day you open,' said the Councillor. 'If you don't last a week, then you lose.'

'And if we do, *you* lose,' said Dad, shaking Trusscot's hand.

Mr Trusscot glanced at Oscar who had been watching him suspiciously since he arrived.

'While I'm here,' he said, 'you should keep that dog on a lead. It's for his own good.'

'What do you mean?' asked Sam.

'The Council's had a lot of complaints lately about stray dogs causing a nuisance,' said Trusscot. 'So we've decided to take action. Starting this week, we've employed a company to clear them all off the streets.'

Oscar sat up, suddenly alert.

'But what will happen to them?' asked Sam.

'Oh I shouldn't worry, I'm sure they'll be taken care of,' said Trusscot. 'Now I'll leave you to get on – you've obviously got a great deal to do. What are you going to call the place by the way – *The Cockroach Cafe*?'

He went off, shaking his head and squeaking

at his own joke.

Sam thought he wouldn't mind seeing smug-faced Mr Trusscot sitting down to a big bowl of dog food. All the same he couldn't help worrying that his Dad had made a risky bet. At the moment the hut looked like somewhere you'd pay to avoid. He looked around for Oscar and found him waiting by the door.

'I'd better go,' Sam said. 'I think Oscar wants me to take him for a walk.'

Chapter 3

Puppy Love

As Sam and Oscar headed back along Beach Road, a large black van drove slowly past. Sam caught a brief glimpse of two dark brown uniformed figures sitting in the front. At first he thought they were police but then he saw what was written on the side of the van.

K9 Dog Control

Dogs are our business

(Call Ruffley 9247531)

Through a window at the back, Sam caught

sight of a sad-eyed mongrel staring mournfully out. So Trusscot hadn't exaggerated – the Council really did mean to clear all strays off the streets and work had already begun. Oscar broke into a run.

'Come on, we need to hurry,' he said.

Ten minutes later they arrived at a dead-end alley off Ramsey Road. Sam had been here once before and it hadn't improved much. It was still filthy, foul smelling and piled with a sea of rubbish. Oscar raised his head and barked. They waited a few seconds but nothing stirred except a plastic bag in the breeze.

'Maybe they've moved on?' suggested Sam.

Oscar trotted deeper into the alley and barked again. A moment later a cardboard box toppled down from a pile of rubbish. Slowly, two dogs emerged from the heap. They were an odd pair. One was an old boxer dog and the other a little Jack Russell. Both dogs had matted, filthy fur and smelled like they hadn't had a bath since Christmas. Sam remembered Oscar telling him their names were Bingo and Mitzi.

Mitzi was the Jack Russell and she seemed to have put on weight. Sam waited while the dogs went through their usual sniffing greeting and then got down to exchanging news. To him it sounded like a series of barks, yaps and growls, but eventually Oscar broke off to report back.

'Well, good news,' Oscar said. 'As you can see, Mitzi is having puppies.'

'Puppies?' Sam wondered how he could have been so stupid. Mitzi hadn't put on weight at all: she was pregnant! 'That's great!' he exclaimed.

Oscar grunted. 'Not so great if you're sleeping here,' he said. 'And there are men prowling the streets wanting to put you in a van.'

'Oh no, I hadn't thought of that,' admitted Sam.

'Well, luckily, you can help,' Oscar went on. 'You've got a big house with plenty of room.

Bingo and Mitzi just need somewhere to stay for a while.'

Sam looked awkward. 'I'd like to, Oscar, but it's not my house,' he pointed out. 'And I'm pretty sure Mum and Dad won't let me have any more dogs.'

'It's only two more, we're not talking about hundreds!' said Oscar. 'Anyway, one, two or three, what's the difference?'

'A lot of difference, especially if there are going to be puppies,' argued Sam. 'We'd have to look after them.'

Oscar looked back to where Bingo and Mitzi stood, waiting hopefully.

'Okay, maybe you're right,' he admitted. 'It's probably best if we don't tell your parents.'

Back at Sam's house the four of them stood outside, trying to work out the best way to get in. When Oscar had first turned up a few months ago Sam had managed to smuggle him up to his room without his parents knowing. Sneaking in two dogs was far more of a challenge. Bingo was on the large side, Mitzi was heavily pregnant and both dogs stank to high heaven. Sam thought the whole idea was crazy, but he was trying his best to help. He didn't want Oscar's friends to be taken away in a van.

'Stay here and keep out of sight,' he said. 'I'll go in and check that the coast is clear.'

The three dogs trooped into the front garden, hiding among the rose bushes and hydrangeas. Sam had a feeling his Mum wouldn't be very pleased about that. He walked up the path, intending to go round to the back. But he hadn't got far when disaster struck. The front door opened and out came his mum.

'Oh, Sam,' she said. 'I thought you were out with your dad.'

'I was,' said Sam. 'But then Oscar needed a walk.'

His mum frowned. 'Where *is* Oscar?' she asked.

'Oh, he's around somewhere,' said Sam vaguely. He caught sight of Oscar crouching among the bushes. His friends were hiding beside him, although Bingo's bottom stuck up like a giant brown boulder. Sam thought there were probably giraffes that were better at hiding. He wished his mum would hurry up and go wherever she was going.

'What did you think of it then?' she asked.

Sam looked blank.

'The beach cafe?'

'Oh that, yes. It'll be good when it's finished,' said Sam, loyally.

'That bad, eh?' sighed Mum. 'Well I said I'd call in on your gran.'

Sam held his breath as his mum marched down the path. If she happened to look round, she'd see three dogs hiding very badly in the flower beds. Oscar must have realised this because he tried to duck down lower. Unfortunately he trod on Bingo's paw and the Boxer let out a startled yelp. Sam heard a lot of noisy rustling and scuffling in the bushes.

'OSCAR!' cried Mum, sharply. 'Come out of there, now!'

Oscar's head popped up, closely followed by Bingo and Mitzi's anxious faces. Mum folded her arms and gave Sam a stern look.

'Who's this?' she demanded.

Sam looked guilty. 'Just a couple of Oscar's friends,' he said. 'I was wondering if maybe they could . . .'

'NO,' replied Mum. 'Absolutely not.'

'But just for a few days,' pleaded Sam.

'Out of the question,' said Mum. 'I've told you before, we're not a dogs' home and besides, they're probably crawling with fleas.'

'But Mitzi is having . . .'

'SAM!' interrupted Mum. 'I don't know where you found them but they *cannot* stay here!'

Sam sighed. He knew better that to argue with his mum when she put her foot down. It was Oscar's crazy idea to bring his friends to the house but they'd just have to think of somewhere else. They set off again down Beach Road with the dogs trailing behind. Sam kept a keen eye out for the black van just in case it was still on the prowl.

'What we need is somewhere that would be

safe for a while,' he said.

'Yes,' said Oscar. 'Safe and warm – with room for a few puppies.'

'But it has to be empty,' added Sam. 'And where are we going to find somewhere like that?'

Oscar's tail started to wag quickly.

'The beach hut!' he said.

'What? No! They can't live there!' protested Sam.

'Why not?' asked Oscar. 'It's safe, there's room and right now it's empty. It's perfect!'

'But what if my Dad wants to start work on it?' asked Sam.

'Then we'll hide them,' said Oscar. 'It's only for a few days. You wouldn't leave them on the streets, would you? Look at the poor things!'

Sam sighed. Mitzi looked exhausted from all

the walking and hiding in front gardens, while Bingo looked extremely hungry. Sam didn't have any better ideas but he had a feeling that using the beach hut was asking for trouble.

Chapter 4

Home Sweet Bone

The next morning was a Sunday, which in the Shilling house usually meant a long lie-in. However, when he came downstairs, Sam found his dad wearing his blue work overalls and making breakfast.

'Morning, sleepyhead!' he said, brightly. 'How do you fancy helping me with the beach hut today? Clear it all out, so I can start painting.'

Sam gaped. *The beach hut?* That was the last place he wanted to go because Bingo and Mitzi were sleeping there. Dad would go up the wall if he found out his dream cafe was housing a pair of smelly street dogs.

'But it's Sunday,' Sam objected. 'Couldn't we start on it tomorrow?'

'You've got school tomorrow,' said Dad. 'Anyway, I want to get on. I'm aiming to open next weekend to show old Fusspot I mean business.'

Sam's head reeled. He had hoped that the cafe would stand empty for a week or two, giving them some breathing space. If they turned up now who knew what they might find?

He hurried upstairs to break the news to Oscar, who was lazing on the bed.

'What do we do now?' he asked.

'Don't panic,' yawned Oscar. 'No sense in getting your tail in twist.'

'I don't have a tail, Oscar,' said Sam.

Oscar hopped down off the bed and shook himself.

'It's only a shabby old hut, I expect your Dad will be pleased someone's using it,' he said.

'No, he won't! He'll do his nut and I'll get the blame!' said Sam.

'All right, then we'll just have to make sure he doesn't see them,' replied Oscar.

'How do we do that?'

Oscar thought for a moment.

'You keep him busy while I run ahead to warn Bingo and Mitzi,' he said. 'I'll find somewhere to hide them till he's gone.'

'Good idea,' agreed Sam. 'But how do I keep my dad busy?'

'I don't know!' said Oscar. 'I can't think of everything!'

Sam followed him out to the top of the stairs.

'Remember to keep an eye out,' he whispered. 'I don't want them putting you in that van.'

Sam insisted that he and his dad stop and call for Louie on the way. This was partly to give Oscar more time but also because he hoped Louie might be able to help. He quickly filled him in on the situation while Louie searched for his trainers.

Sam didn't explain all the details or that this was all Oscar's idea. Louie didn't know that Oscar had ideas, let alone that he could put them into words. Nevertheless he seemed to find the whole thing exciting, especially the bit about opening a beach cafe. He wanted to know if they'd be serving chocolate milkshake and would Sam be getting free drinks?

As they came in sight of the beach hut, Sam spotted Oscar outside the door. He scampered back inside quickly. Luckily Dad hadn't noticed but Sam worried they were arriving too soon. He tried to think of some reason to delay.

'Oh Louie, you forgot!' he said, halting suddenly.

Louie looked puzzled. 'Forgot what?'

'You know, that thing, the thing you were

going to bring,' said Sam, nodding meaningfully. 'We'll have to go back.'

Louie frowned. 'What thing?'

'You know, your . . . football,' said Sam at random. 'We left it at your house.'

'I know,' replied Louie. 'But I thought we were looking at your dad's cafe, not playing football.'

'Exactly and we've wasted enough time already, so let's get on,' said Dad, marching ahead impatiently.

Sam threw up his hands. 'Great, thanks a lot,' he said. 'I was trying to give them time to hide.'

'Who?'

'The dogs of course!' said Sam.

'Oh, I see!' cried Louie. 'Well why didn't you say so instead of going on about football?'

They found Oscar waiting for them outside the beach hut. Dad looked surprised to see him.

'Hello, Oscar,' he said. 'When did you get here?'

Inside, the wooden hut looked just the same, apart from the blanket and the pile of cushions lying in the middle of the floor. Bingo and Mitzi evidently weren't in the habit of tidying up.

'Isn't this one of ours?' asked Dad, picking up a cushion. 'What's it doing here?'

Sam shrugged. 'Don't ask me. Maybe mum brought them,' he said.

'Or maybe cushion burglars broke into your house and stole them in the night,' suggested Louie.

Sam rolled his eyes at him. This was what happened when you asked Louie to help.

'Ugh! It stinks,' said Dad. 'And it's covered

in hairs. By the look of it something's been sleeping here.'

'Who'd want to sleep here?' asked Sam, innocently.

'Probably a dog or a fox,' said Dad. 'They look like animal hairs.'

Dad began searching the hut for any sign of the intruders. Louie silently mouthed, *Where are they?* but Sam shook his head. He hadn't the faintest clue where Bingo and Mitzi were – he only hoped Oscar had hidden them well. It didn't take long to find out.

Sam found his dad in the back room where it smelled of damp. The rusty cooker and the sink sat side by side next to a tiny broom cupboard in the corner.

'Well anyway, there's no one here,' said Sam, relieved.

'Not now obviously,' said Dad, trying to open a window.

Out of curiosity, Sam opened the door to the broom cupboard. Inside were Bingo and Mitzi,

squashed on top of each other like two halves of a sandwich. Sam slammed the door shut quickly – too quickly.

'What's in there?' asked Dad, looking round.

'Nothing!' said Sam. 'Just . . . um . . . cobwebs and nothingness.'

Dad gave him a funny look and wiped his finger across the dust. If he opens the door now, thought Sam, Bingo and Mitzi will probably fall out on top of him. Sam prayed that they wouldn't make a sound or decide they needed the toilet. Luckily, just then, Louie came to the rescue.

'Look at this!' he called. Next door he'd found a small silver coin, jammed in a gap between the floorboards.

'Do you think it's Roman?' he asked, hopefully.

'I doubt it, it's a sixpence,' said Dad. He looked around. 'We'll have to get rid of all this junk. I'll go and fetch the car. You two could sweep the floor if you can find a broom anywhere.'

Sam waited till he'd disappeared and breathed a sigh of relief.

'That was close,' he groaned.

'Was it?' said Louie. 'Where are they then?'

Sam led him next door and opened the broom cupboard. Bingo and Mitzi tumbled out, glad to escape. Bingo licked Sam's hand gratefully while Mitzi rubbed against his legs.

'I've always wanted a puppy,' said Louie, crouching down beside them.

'What about your house, then?' asked Sam. 'You could take them for a bit.'

'I've told you before, we've got hamsters,' said Louie.

'Well they can't stay here with my dad coming back,' said Sam. 'We'll have to find somewhere else.'

Oscar took the two dogs outside to get some fresh air, while Sam found a brush in the broom cupboard and they tried to sweep the floor. They hadn't got very far when a loud commotion outside interrupted them. It sounded like Oscar barking furiously.

Sam rushed outside in time to see the black K9 van parked a little way down the road. A barrel-shaped man in a brown uniform was trying to shut the back doors. Oscar jumped up, barking wildly and getting in his way. Sam felt a wave of panic.

'HEY, STOP! That's my dog!' he yelled, racing towards the van. But the warden slammed the back door shut. Glancing back

at Sam, he jumped into the passenger seat. Seconds later the black van drove off at speed, screeching away in a cloud of dust.

Sam didn't need to ask Oscar to know who was inside. It was Bingo and Mitzi – they'd lost them.

Chapter 5

Follow that Van!

Oscar padded along beside Sam sunk in gloomy silence. They'd left Louie at his house and were heading home.

Oscar hadn't said a word. He hadn't even stopped to sniff any lampposts on the way.

'They'll be all right, though won't they?' said Sam.

'All right?' he snorted. 'You saw what just happened. They're kidnappers! Even worse, dognappers!'

'I know,' said Sam. 'But you heard Trusscot, that's what the Council's paying them to do.

Anyway there's not much we can do about it.'

'We can rescue them,' said Oscar. 'If it was Louie would you let him be carted off in a black van?'

'Well, no,' admitted Sam.

'And Mitzi could have her puppies are any day now,' Oscar went on. 'I promised to take care of them.'

Sam nodded glumly. He'd never seen a dog give birth to puppies but he knew Mitzi ought to be somewhere safe and warm.

'The trouble is we've no idea where they are,' he pointed out.

Oscar thought this over for a moment. His tail was still for a moment then thumped like mad when an idea came to him. It was doing it now.

'The van!' he said. 'If we follow the van it'll

lead us to them.'

'Yes, but it's gone,' said Sam.

'It'll be back soon, I'd bet my dinner on it,' said Oscar. 'They'll be looking for more dogs so all I have to do is hang around on the road.'

'You?' said Sam.

'Yes, I'm a dog in case you've forgotten,' said Oscar.

'But you're *my* dog, you're not a stray,' argued Sam. 'What if they try to put you in the van?'

'They won't – not if you're there to stop them,' said Oscar. 'Then as soon as the van drives off we can follow and find out where they go.'

Sam looked unconvinced. 'We'd need to be on bikes or we'd lose them,' he said.

Oscar nodded. 'Bikes, yes, good idea, I don't think I've ever ridden one.'

Later that afternoon, they met Louie on Beach Road. Sam had borrowed his mum's bike because it had a basket at the front, which Oscar could fit in at a tight squeeze. Oscar was wearing a fur-lined pilot's hat that he'd found in Sam's cupboard. He claimed it would keep his ears warm, though Sam reckoned it was just an excuse to wear a hat.

'Well where do we start then?' asked Louie.

Sam had no idea. The K9 van might be anywhere in town or it might not return at all. All they could do was hang around on Beach Road, hoping that the van would eventually turn up.

They waited for what seem like hours, seeing only a few cars and old Mrs Porter taking her little Pekinese for a walk. Sam and Louie hid round the corner with their bikes. Oscar trotted up and down making himself obvious, which wasn't too difficult for a dog in a hat.

'This is a waste of time, it obviously isn't coming,' grumbled Louie.

But just then they saw Oscar stiffen and raise his head. Sam heard the engine first, then he saw the black van turn the corner at the far end of the road. Spotting Oscar on the street, a woman poked her head out of the window.

'Slow down, Harry, we might be in luck,' she said.

The van slowed to a halt. Sam knew they had to move fast or Oscar was in trouble.

The two of them came flying round the corner on their bikes and jammed on their brakes. Sam sprang off and knelt beside Oscar, slipping a lead over his head.

The warden locked eyes with him and her smile disappeared.

'False alarm,' she said, rapping on the van door. 'Drive on, Harry.'

They waited till the van was a short way down the road and set off, pedalling like fury. Sam bent over his handlebars while Oscar bumped up and down in the basket like a sack of potatoes. They followed the van for a mile or

two as it criss-crossed the back streets of town. Luckily it wasn't going at full speed as it was looking for strays. On the outskirts of town, the van dipped down a hill and went under a railway bridge. Sam and Louie sped after it but when they emerged on the other side, the van had vanished completely. Sam skidded to a halt and Oscar almost shot out of the basket like a cork from a bottle. He turned and gave Sam a withering look.

'Sorry,' Sam said. 'I forgot.'

The road stretched away for miles with no sign of any van. Oscar jumped down and sniffed around, trying to pick up the scent. Then he barked and set off running down a narrow lane that branched away to the left. They soon noticed deep tyre tracks in the mud.

At the end of the lane they came to a wooden gate with a muddy yard beyond. An old red brick barn stood to one side. Sam and Louie got off their bikes. Somewhere across the yard they could hear barking and yapping. The sign on the gate said: PRIVATE PROPERTY – KEEP OUT! STRICTLY NO CALLERS!

'What now?' asked Louie. 'Shall we ring the doorbell?'

Sam crept forward to the gate with Oscar beside him. He could see the black van parked in the yard. Leaning against it were the two wardens drinking from mugs. They made an odd pair. The one called Harry had a shaved head and was round as a beach ball. His partner was a sharp-faced woman with black hair and long red fingernails. Harry looked up and caught sight of them.

'OI! What do you fink you're doing?' he yelled.

He came running towards them, waving his mug.

'This is private property! Can't you read?' he cried.

'It's all right, Harry, leave this to me,' said the woman, arriving swiftly.

She gave them a practiced smile. 'My name's Carla,' she said. 'We passed you earlier down on the seafront, didn't we? So how can we help you boys?'

Sam looked at Louie, unsure where to begin.

'We're looking for some dogs,' he said. 'I think you might have picked them up this morning by mistake.'

Harry folded his arms. 'I don't fink so,' he growled.

'It's all right,' said Carla. 'We take in a lot of dogs for their own good. Can you describe them?'

'A boxer and a Jack Russell,' answered Sam.

'Bingo and Mitzi – she's having puppies,' added Louie.

'Puppies? Oh we *adore* puppies, don't we Harry?' cooed Carla.

'Yeah, love 'em,' said Harry, revealing a gold tooth.

'These dogs though – are they actually yours?' asked Carla.

'Well no, not exactly,' admitted Sam. 'But we know them.'

'They're friends of Oscar's,' explained Louie, pointing to him. 'So we just want to check they're okay.'

'Of course you do.' Carla smiled again and her red fingernails tapped the gate impatiently. 'But you have to understand the dogs we take in are living on the streets. When they come to us we bathe them, feed them and look after them, isn't that right, Harry?'

'Couldn't be righter,' agreed Harry.

Sam and Louie looked at each other, unsure what to say.

'So you see, if your friends are here then they're in good hands,' said Carla. 'Nice to meet you.'

The two wardens turned away but Oscar

wasn't leaving.

'Could we see them?' Sam called out.

'Carla looked round. 'I'm sorry, visitors aren't allowed,' she said. 'Regulations.'

'Yeah relegations, see?' echoed Harry.

'But you're welcome to look in on our reception room,' offered Carla. She opened the gate and led them over to a small window in the brick barn. Inside Sam could see a warmly lit room where a spaniel lay sleeping peacefully on a beanbag.

'You see?' said Carla. 'Better than a four – star hotel.'

They left soon after, bumping their bikes back down the potholed lane.

'Well, she seemed nice,' said Louie.

'Yes,' agreed Sam. 'At least we know they're looking after them.'

Oscar didn't turn round but Sam thought he could tell from his back what he was thinking. *Believe me*, it said, *this isn't over yet.*

Chapter 6

In the Soup

Back home that evening, Oscar waited until everyone had gone to bed. He hopped up onto the duvet and settled into his usual spot. Sam put out the light.

'So obviously we'll have to go back,' said Oscar.

The light went back on.

'What for?' asked Sam.

Oscar twitched his nose. 'I don't trust them,' he said. 'There's a funny smell about the place.'

'It smelled okay to me,' said Sam. 'And surely it's better than Bingo and Mitzi living on the streets? They'll look after her while she has her puppies.'

Oscar blinked. 'How do you know?' he demanded.

'Well, because they told us.'

'And if I told you I had wings you'd think that was true?'

'Of course not!' said Sam.

'There you are then,' said Oscar. 'Truth is like an old bone – sometimes you have to dig it up.'

Sam pulled a face. 'What does that mean?' he asked.

'It means we have to go back,' said Oscar.

He closed his eyes as if that settled the matter. Sam lay down under the duvet and sighed. He couldn't see what bones had to do with it but there was no use in arguing with Oscar, who was always convinced he was right. Sam was never sure if he was right, mainly because he often turned out to be wrong. All the same he wasn't in a hurry to return to the yard – he was pretty sure they wouldn't be welcome.

In any case, the next day he had other things on his mind, because he suddenly got a job. Dad surprised them by announcing the Toast Cafe would open for a trial run on Wednesday evening. Not everything was finished, he admitted, but he wanted to try out the menu on a few invited friends and neighbours. The only thing lacking was a waiter, which was where Sam came in. Sam had never waited in his life (apart from at a bus stop) but since Dad was offering to pay *double pocket money*, he didn't take much persuasion.

At six o'clock when Sam and Oscar arrived it was a warm summer's evening. A few of the neighbours sat around at a jumble of wooden tables outside the cafe. The beach hut had been painted white and the roof repaired so it looked less like an elephant had sat on it.

Sam found his Dad inside, wearing a chef's apron and looking rather flustered. Cups, plates and bowls were piled high in the sink.

Thick brown soup bubbled in a saucepan while a tower of toast sat on a plate, growing cold.

'Thank goodness you're here,' said Dad. 'I've been rushing around like a madman. Can you get out there and start taking people's orders?'

'Okay,' said Sam. 'But what do I do exactly?'

'There's nothing to it, just ask them what they want,' said Dad, handing him a notebook. 'As long as it's on toast, write it down. Remember to be polite and for heaven's sake keep Oscar away from the customers.'

'I thought he could help,' said Sam.

'It's a cafe, Sam,' sighed Dad. 'Dogs and cafes just don't mix.'

Oscar walked off.

Outside, Sam hung back, feeling a little nervous. He had hoped his dad would give him a bit of time to practice. Still, at least he had

Oscar to keep him company. He decided to start with his mum who was sitting nearby.

'Ah, a waiter at last,' she smiled. 'I don't know what your dad's playing at, some of his customers are getting impatient.'

'I think it's maybe harder than he thought,' said Sam. 'Anyway, what can I get you – please?' he added, remembering he had to be polite.

'Just coffee and a slice of cake,' said Mum.

Sam's pencil hovered. 'Cake? Um I'm not sure we've got any,' he said.

'It's a cafe, you must have cake!' said Mum.

'We've got toast,' said Sam, pointing to the menu. 'Cheese on toast, beans on toast, egg on toast . . .'

'I had toast for breakfast,' said Mum. 'I'll have a cappuccino with a chocolate brownie, please.'

'Right er . . . thank you,' said Sam starting to write. 'How do you spell cappo-thingummy?'

'Never mind,' sighed Mum. 'Just a coffee. Now you better serve Mr Trusscot before he explodes.'

Sam hurried over to the next table. He was surprised Dad had invited their fusspot neighbour. Trusscot was probably only there because he wanted to make sure he'd win the bet. Sitting with him was a woman with glasses and a solemn expression. Sam thought she was a bit young to be Mr Trusscot's girlfriend. In any case she didn't look that mad.

'Hi! I mean, good evening, what can I get you, please?' asked Sam.

Trusscot checked his watch. 'Thirteen minutes, seven seconds – that's how long we've been waiting,' he complained. 'In that time I could have walked home and made my own tea.'

'Thank you,' said Sam, sticking to politeness. 'Would you like tea and toast?'

'There doesn't seem to be much else on the

menu,' grumbled Trusscot. 'Tea in a teapot, no teabags, no sugar and ideally before I die of thirst.'

Sam wrote this in his notebook. He couldn't remember all the details so he just wrote *Toast, tea – dying of thirst!* adding a smiley face. He looked up.

'This is Mrs Smedley,' said Trusscot. 'I thought she'd be interested to see your so-called cafe.'

'How old are you?' asked Mrs Smedley. 'Aren't you still at school?'

'No, school finishes at half past three,' Sam answered truthfully.

Mrs Smedley sniffed. 'You're rather young for a waiter,' she said. 'And this is your dog, is it?'

Sam had forgotten Oscar who was standing close to Mr Trusscot watching him in case he stole a teaspoon.

'This is Oscar, he's helping me take the orders,' smiled Sam.

'Hmm. I see,' grunted Mrs Smedley. She wrote something down in a small black book. Sam wondered if she was a reporter from the *Bunting News*. A new cafe was obviously big news.

'I'll have the soup, what sort do you have?' she asked.

'Brown,' answered Sam.

'Brown?'

'Yes, thank you. Would you like toast with it?' asked Sam. 'We've got cheese on toast, egg on toast . . .'

'Just soup, thank you very much,' said Mrs Smedley, making another note in her book. Sam decided he better give his dad the orders before he got them muddled.

'Chocolate brownie?' said Dad. 'Why on earth did you offer them that?'

'I didn't,' said Sam. 'Mum asked for it. You said write down whatever they say.'

'Yes but we're serving toast, not cakes,' said Dad. 'I've got stacks of it.'

'I tried my best,' said Sam. He didn't see how he could be polite and force toast down people's throats at the same time.

'Anyway, Mr Trusscot wants toast and a pot of tea before he dies,' Sam reported. 'And his friend wants the soup.'

'Trusscot?' said Dad. 'What's Miseryface doing here? I didn't invite him! And who's this friend?'

'Don't ask me, but she's writing stuff down,' said Sam. 'Maybe she's from the newspaper?'

Dad went to the door and peered out. 'If I

know Trusscot he's up to something,' he said, darkly. 'You better take them their food.'

Sam hurried out, carrying a tray and trying not to trip over Oscar. Some of Mr Trusscot's tea spilled out of the pot.

'Finally!' sighed Mr Trusscot. 'The service in this place is beyond a joke.'

'I'm trying my best. I haven't had much practice,' said Sam.

He set down the tea and the bowl of thick, brown soup. Trusscot seemed to be searching under the table for something. He finally sat up.

'Would you like salt?' he asked his companion.

'Just a pinch,' said Mrs Smedley.

Trusscot made a big deal of shaking the salt pot, taking his time. Sam was about to move onto the next table when disaster struck. He caught sight of something small and black, swimming in the soup. A fly! How it had got there he couldn't think – he didn't remember seeing it before. Luckily Mrs Smedley was buttering her bread roll and hadn't spotted it yet. Sam had to do something quickly. He grabbed the bowl.

'Sorry this is too hot, I'll take it back,' he mumbled.

'Don't be ridiculous, put it down!' snapped Trusscot.

Sam dithered. Any moment now one of them would notice the fly. He seized a spoon from the table and plunged it into the soup. With a flick of his wrist he managed to catapult the fly so it shot out like a bullet. It worked – or at least it almost worked. It was just bad luck that the fly landed on Mr Trusscot's shirt. It stuck there fast in a splodge of brown soup.

'Oh dear!' said Sam.

Mr Trusscot looked down and saw it. He leapt to his feet.

'ARGHH! ARE YOU TRYING TO KILL ME?' he yelled, brushing the fly off as if it was a scorpion.

'Sorry,' said Sam. 'It's gone now – thank you.'

But Trusscot was hopping mad. He pushed back his chair.

'That's it!' he fumed. 'That is the final straw!'

The other diners were all turning round to stare. Mum was trying not to laugh while Dad had come rushing out to see what the noise was about.

'You call this a cafe?' Trusscot cried. 'It's a disgrace! Hopeless service, dogs running in and out and dead insects in the soup!'

'Actually, it's not dead,' Sam pointed out. 'Look, I think it's still moving!'

Trusscot glared and turned to his dining companion.

'Well I trust you've seen enough, Mrs Smedley?' he said.

Mrs Smedley had. She gathered up her notebook.

'Don't think you've heard the last of this, Shilling,' warned Trusscot. 'We'll be back on your opening night and then we'll see! You just wait!'

He turned to storm out, but had to step over Oscar who was licking the soup on the floor.

'AND PUT YOUR DRATTED DOG ON A LEAD!' yelled Trusscot.

Chapter 7

Nosing Around

Back home that evening, Mum made hot chocolate and put out a plate of flapjacks and biscuits.

'Never mind, love,' she said. 'It wasn't a total disaster. At least a few people came.'

Dad shook his head. 'It would have been fine without that numskull, Trusscot. Now he'll go round telling everyone we poison our customers.'

'I don't know where the fly came from,' said Sam.

'It's not your fault, Sam,' smiled Mum. 'Anyway it was quite funny.'

'And it doesn't change a thing,' said Dad. 'We open next Saturday. If old Fusspot thinks he's won our bet he can forget it.'

Mum raised an eyebrow.

'Ah yes, the bet, you forgot to mention that,' she said.

'Oh, well, it's nothing really,' said Dad.

'Mr Trusscot bet Dad that the cafe won't last a week,' grinned Sam. 'And guess what – the loser has to eat a bowl of dog food!'

Mum's eyebrows shot up. 'Seriously?' she said. 'You'd better not lose then.'

'I don't intend to,' said Dad.

'Well I hate to say it but the cafe's nowhere near ready,' said Mum. 'I waited half an hour for a cup of coffee. What if Fusspot's friend writes about that in the newspaper?'

'Oh, Lord!' said Dad.

'Exactly, so for starters you'll need a proper menu and more people serving the customers,' said Mum.

'I know, but where am I going to find anyone?' asked Dad.

Mum folded her arms. 'Well you could always ask me,' she said. 'I can bake cakes and wait at tables, at least until you get going.'

'Would you?' said Dad.

'Of course I would, we can't let old Fusspot win can we?' laughed Mum. 'Here's to the Toast Cafe!' They all raised their mugs while Sam dropped a biscuit under the table for Oscar.

He didn't know why Dad hadn't asked Mum to help before. He was great at having ideas but about as organised as a sock drawer. What's more, Mum could actually cook without setting fire to things.

The next day, down at the beach, Oscar returned to the subject of Bingo and Mitzi. He said he'd promised on dog's honour to help them. Sam had never heard of dog's honour but he guessed it mattered if you were a dog. All the same he wasn't keen.

'I don't know, Oscar,' he said. 'We can't just turn up at that place and start nosing around.'

'I can,' said Oscar. 'No one pays dogs any attention, especially if the yard is full of them. I could slip in and find my friends before anyone sees me.'

Oscar made it sound simple – like popping down the shops to get some milk. On the other hand, most shops didn't have big signs saying *Keep Out*.

When they reached the end of the lane the sun was low in the sky. Sam hid his bike among the trees and they crept round the barn to a barbed wire fence. The black van was parked in the yard but otherwise the place seemed deserted.

'You stay here, while I have a nose around,' said Oscar.

'But what if they see you?' worried Sam. 'They might put you in with the others.'

'They'll have to catch me first,' said Oscar with a wink. He wriggled under the barbed wire fence and looked back a last time. 'If anyone comes make a noise and try to keep them busy,' he said.

'What?' said Sam. 'Oscar, wait!'

But it was too late. Oscar had vanished into

the shadows.

Sam waited, crouched in the damp grass, feeling uneasy. He wished that Louie had come so that at least he would have had someone to talk to. What if Oscar was caught? There might be secret cameras or even guard dogs (although that seemed less likely).

Suddenly the silence was broken by a wild bedlam of barking that came from across the yard. Sam guessed it was Oscar – the other dogs must have seen him.

A door banged open and the two wardens came running out of a small hut.

'What the devil's going on?' cried Carla.

'Beats me, they're always barking about something,' said Harry.

'Better check on them,' said Carla. 'Bring your bat, just in case.'

Sam's heart raced. Oscar was in trouble unless Sam could warn him somehow. 'Keep them busy,' Oscar said, but how was he meant to do that? Sam looked around, trying to think. There was only the van parked on a slope in the yard. Suddenly Oscsar had a brainwave.

Crawling under the barbed wire, Sam ran, keeping in the shadow of the barn. Harry returned, carrying a cricket bat and the two wardens headed off in the direction of the barking. Sam knew he didn't have long. He scrambled over to the van and tried the door. It was unlocked and he slipped inside.

WOOP! WOOP! WOOP!

Help! He hadn't counted on the van having an alarm! Any moment now the wardens would come running back. His hands shook as he tried to remember how his parents started the car at home. Turn the keys, he thought. But there weren't any. Put the car in wotsit and then take off . . . the handbrake – of course!

Voices were coming back this way. He gripped the metal handbrake and tugged. It wouldn't budge. He pushed in a button and yanked it with both hands. This time it gave way with a creak. The van lurched backwards. Sam fell out of the side door with the alarm still ringing in his ears. Scrambling to his feet, he pushed

the van as hard as he could. He felt it start to roll. As the two wardens appeared, he darted back into the shadows and lay flat on his belly, panting.

'THE VAN!' shouted Harry.

'I'm not deaf!' said Carla.

Harry pointed. 'No, Carla, it's moving! Look!'

Harry was right. The van was rolling backwards down the slope, gently at first but now gaining speed. More to the point, it was coming straight towards them.

'LOOK OUT!' squawked Carla as they threw themselves to the side, just in time.

The van shot between them, bumping along with one door flapping open. It would have kept going except for the metal water trough in the middle of the yard. The van hit it with an ear-splitting crash, toppling it over. A tidal wave of brown murky water swept across the yard as the alarm finally gave up woop-wooping and fell silent.

'You great blockhead!' groaned Carla. 'You

left the handbrake off!'

Sam blinked. The van's back bumper was dented and the yard was awash with muddy water. It had all worked better than he'd expected. A minute later Oscar appeared and wriggled back under the wire to join him.

'Well, you seem to have kept them busy,' he said. 'Shall we get going?'

CHAPTER 8

GHOST DOG

The next day dawned with a fine mist hanging over the town. It was Saturday, the day of the Toast Cafe's grand opening. The leaflets had gone out and Mr Shilling was certain the weather would brighten up soon. All they had to do now was wait for the crowds to arrive.

Sam went down to the cafe with Oscar after breakfast. The beach hut had been transformed in the last few days. Now it looked like a proper cafe rather than a Scout hut with a leaky roof. Inside a new cooker gleamed and the sink sparkled. Mum had covered the outside tables

in pale blue cloths while over the entrance fairy lights twinkled. A delicious smell came from trays of muffins, brownies, and flapjacks, which Mum had made for customers who didn't want toast. A blackboard welcomed customers in.

Sam looked up and down the road for signs of people. A caravan dawdled past and a jogger ran by on the beach. Overhead the seagulls wheeled and cried; otherwise it was as deadly quiet as a maths exam.

'It's early yet, you wait till eleven,' said Dad, peering out of the door.

Sam and Oscar exchanged looks as he disappeared inside.

'What happens at eleven?' asked Oscar.

'Well that's when people often have a coffee break,' explained Sam.

'Right,' said Oscar. 'And they all go out to cafes?'

'Well, no, not always,' admitted Sam. 'Some make their own coffee and then others don't like coffee at all. Also there are three other cafes in town.'

Oscar's ears flopped. 'Hmm,' he said. 'Maybe your Dad was wrong.'

'About what?' asked Sam.

'That cafes and dogs don't mix,' replied Oscar. 'You should think about it.'

He trotted up the road and came back. 'No one's coming, we've still got time,' he said.

Sam sighed. 'Oscar, I can't! I promised Dad I'd help.'

Sam didn't need to ask what Oscar had in mind. After their visit to the yard Oscar had told him what he'd seen. It wasn't good news. Bingo and Mitzi were kept cooped up in a cage with half a dozen other dogs. There were five or six pens of dogs with scarcely room to move. Evidently Carla and Harry had been telling whopping lies. Worst of all, Mitzi looked like she might give birth any day. Time was running out.

'We could be back in an hour,' said Oscar. 'Oodles of time.'

'You'll get me in trouble,' said Sam. 'Anyway you said they keep the cages locked. How would we get them out?'

'Leave that to me,' said Oscar. 'We'll need to borrow a bag of your mum's cake powder.'

'Cake powder?' repeated Sam.

Just then Louie arrived on his bike.

'Hey, I just bumped into Mrs Porter,' he said, breathlessly. 'You know she's got that little dog?'

'Pinky,' said Sam.

'Yes, well now she hasn't,' said Louie. 'He's disappeared.'

'What? When did this happen?' asked Sam.

'Last night – he went out and never came back,' said Louie. 'No sign of him this morning. She sounded pretty upset.'

Sam met Oscar's eyes and guessed what he was thinking – the black van. But surely Pinky wouldn't have been taken? He was a pet Pekinese, not a stray living on the streets. Mrs Porter lived on Sam's street and he knew Pinky meant everything to her. He looked at his watch.

'We'll need our bikes,' he said.

Louie looked confused. 'I thought you were helping your dad this morning,' he said.

'I am, that's why we need to hurry,' said Sam.

When they reached the yard, the buildings

were cloaked in grey mist. The van wasn't there but Sam guessed the yard wouldn't be left unguarded.

'What now then?' whispered Louie.

'We need the keys and they're probably in that hut,' said Sam. 'But don't worry, Oscar's got an idea.'

'Oscar?' said Louie.

'I mean, I've got an idea,' Sam corrected himself. He'd have to be more careful or Louie would start to suspect something.

They crawled under the barbed wire and ran across the yard to the hut. Sam raised his head to peer through a small, dirty window. Inside he could see the warden called Harry sprawled on a sofa.

'You're sure about this?' whispered Sam.

'Me?' asked Louie.

'No, never mind,' said Sam, who'd actually been talking to Oscar.

He brought out the bag of white flour (or cake powder) he'd borrowed from the beach hut. Oscar shut his eyes while Sam emptied the whole bag over him, dusting him from nose to tail. Oscar sneezed – he was now as pale as snow.

'Are you nuts?' asked Louie.

'Shh! Keep your voice down!' whispered Sam.

There was no time to explain and he wasn't sure he could anyway. Oscar padded off on his mission.

Sam stood on tiptoe to trying to see through the window. Harry lay on the sofa with his mouth open, snoring. A half-eaten bag of crisps sat on the floor. The only light came from the small window and the flickering TV screen.

THUMP!

Harry sat up with a start and fell off the sofa.

'Carla?' he said, getting up. 'Carla, is that you?'

A sudden gust of wind made the door bang. Harry stood up slowly, clutching a cushion for protection.

'HELLO?' he said, peering out into the eerie,

grey mist. 'Who's that? Carla, this isn't funny!'

No answer. He shook his head and went to close the door. Turning round, his blood froze and his knees turned to jelly. There was something sitting in the shadows: a white hound or possibly a werewolf, staring at him with piercing black eyes. He must be dreaming.

He walloped himself with the cushion, hoping to wake up.

'SIT DOWN,' barked Oscar.

The white werewolf thing spoke! Harry fell back into an armchair. This *had* to be a bad dream. He should never have had that cheese sandwich earlier.

'I am Ghost Dog,' said Oscar, tall and upright. 'You know why I'm here?'

Harry shook his head.

'I am sent to punish creatures like you,' said Oscar. 'You must pay for your cruelty to dog-kind.'

Harry whimpered. He didn't want to be punished. He was too young to die and he hadn't even finished his crisps. He sunk down on his knees.

'Please, I never meant nothing,' he begged. 'I was just doing my job! I like dogs really, even poodles . . .'

'SILENCE!' barked Ghost Dog, cutting him off. 'If you wish to live, do exactly as I say . . .'

Outside the window, Sam could only see Oscar's white back. Harry seemed to be down on his knees praying or pleading. Sam couldn't see much in the dark room and the TV drowned out whatever they were saying. This was probably just as well as Louie was trying to look over his shoulder.

Back inside, Oscar was giving orders. 'The keys on your belt, take them off and throw them here.'

Harry meekly did as he was told. The keys landed with a thud.

'Now lie on the floor, face down,' said Oscar.

'Like this?' asked Harry.

'Good. Shut your eyes and do not move or get

up. Start counting to a thousand – backwards,'
said Oscar.

Harry wasn't sure he could count backwards,
counting forwards was hard enough, but he
didn't want to die.

'One thousand,' he began. 'One thousand . . .
nine hundred and um . . .'

At the window, Sam and Louie had lost sight
of Oscar. They heard a patter of feet and he
appeared again, like a ghost out of the mist. In
his mouth was a set of keys.

'You got them, nice work!' said Sam.

'Wait, will someone please tell me what's
going on?' said Louie.

'Later, there isn't time,' Sam told him. 'We've
got to find Mitzi and Bingo.'

Oscar knew the way and led them to the rear

of the yard. Inside another barn they found five
or six wire cages full of hungry looking dogs.
Bingo and Mitzi were in the second one but
there was a surprise in store. Three sleepy-eyed
little puppies with white paws and snub noses
snuggled up to their mother. Sam could see they

were a cross between boxers and Jack Russells, which possibly made them Jack Brussels. His heart thumped as he wrestled with the keys, trying to find the right one. Finally the padlock clicked and he swung back the gate. The dogs came pouring out with Bingo in front.

'Awww! Look at the little guys!' cried Louie, scooping up the puppies.

Oscar was staring at the other cages where the dogs were pushing against the gates.

Sam hesitated – they couldn't just leave them. All the same there were five more cages and he had no idea which key fit the locks. He worked feverishly on the next padlock, trying the keys one by one. Finally, he reached the last cage where a small Pekinese looked up at him and yapped excitedly.

'Pinky, is that you?' cried Sam.

'So that's your game, is it?'

Sam froze. He turned round slowly to see Harry, now armed with a cricket bat in one hand. At some point Sam guessed he must have opened his eyes and noticed the trail of dusty white paw prints crossing the floor. Now he stood in the open doorway, blocking their escape.

'Give me the keys,' he snarled. 'And all these dogs, they go back in their pens before I make them.'

The dogs milled around Sam and Louie – there were thirty or more of them.

Sam softly turned the key in the last padlock and felt it spring open. Then he tossed the bunch of keys at Harry's feet. The slow-witted warden stooped to pick them up. That gave Oscar the few seconds he needed. He flew at him, sinking his teeth into Harry's trouser leg and the soft ankle inside.

'ARRGH! LEGGO, you filthy brute!' howled Harry, hopping around with Oscar attached to his foot. He swung the cricket bat aiming to land a blow but it never connected because Bingo's paws caught him in the chest, sending him flying backwards.

'Right, that's it!' panted Harry, raising himself on one knee. 'You want to play rough, eh? Well you asked for it.'

But as he got to his feet the last cage door was barged open. Oscar barked and led his hairy troop forward in a wild stampede. All Harry saw was a mass of fur, paws and teeth before he disappeared beneath the scrum and was trampled underfoot.

Five minutes later, Sam and Louie were
bumping down the lane for the last time. Mitzi
was crammed into Sam's basket along with her

puppies. Oscar and Bingo ran behind, followed by Pinky and the noisy pack of escaped dogs.

Sam glanced behind to make sure no one was following.

'Well, we did it,' he said.

'Yes, but what are we going to do with all these dogs?' asked Louie. 'There are millions of them!'

'Don't ask me,' said Sam. 'Can you stay with Oscar and the others? I need to get back before I'm in trouble.'

'Hang on,' said Louie. 'You still haven't explained how Oscar got those keys. What was he doing in there and why was he covered in flour?'

'Oh right, yes, I'll er . . . tell you later,' promised Sam.

He pedalled off quickly before Louie could

ask any more questions. To be honest he wasn't sure that he would ever be able to explain. The only one who really knew how they'd pulled off the rescue was Oscar – and he wasn't telling.

Chapter 9

Early Closing

Back at the cafe, Sam lifted Mitzi and the puppies out of the bike basket, setting them down carefully by a table. He stared. Something was obviously wrong. He'd expected to find his parents busily serving customers, but the only person there was Mrs Porter sipping a cup of tea. Mum and Dad sat waiting glumly outside while Mr Trusscot was there wearing a look of triumph.

He looked up as Sam came in.

'Ah, I'm afraid you're too late,' he said, gleefully. 'This cafe is about to close.'

'What? We've only just opened!' said Sam.

Dad didn't even ask Sam where he'd been or how he'd come by the puppies.

'You remember Mrs Smedley?' he said. 'It turns out she isn't a reporter after all, she's a health inspector.'

'She's inside now going through the cupboards and poking in the bins,' said Mum.

'But she can't close us down!' protested Sam.

Trusscot gave a laugh. 'I'm afraid that's where you're wrong,' he smirked. 'Every new cafe has to have a health inspection. It's the law. If you fail the inspection then you can't serve food – it's as simple as that.'

Sam couldn't believe it. He was bursting to tell his parents what they'd discovered at the yard but clearly this wasn't the time. Trusscot had planned this whole thing from the start, thought Sam. He was the one who brought Mrs Smedley along in the first place without breathing a word about her job. He'd waited quite deliberately until their opening day to spring his sneaky little surprise. Now their hard work would count for nothing – all because Trusscot was determined to win the bet.

Mrs Smedley finally emerged from the kitchen and they all stood up.

'Well I've carried out a very thorough inspection,' she said.

'We are so grateful, Mrs Smedley,' gushed Trusscot. 'So tell me, what did they fail on? Was it the general filth or the rats in the kitchen?'

'The only rat round here is you,' muttered Dad.

'Well you will need to put in an air extractor,' said Mrs Smedley. 'But apart from that, it's all in order, you've passed.'

Sam cheered and punched the air. For a moment he thought his dad was going to kiss Mrs Smedley, but thankfully he controlled himself. Mr Trusscot, meanwhile, looked like a shiny pink balloon that had just been punctured.

'Passed?' he spluttered. 'How . . . what do you mean?'

'I mean it's a great improvement since my first visit,' said Mrs Smedley. 'You must have all worked very hard.'

'Thank you, we did,' said Mum. 'Now if you'll excuse us, Mr Trusscot, we have a cafe to run. Mrs Smedley, can I offer you a coffee?'

But Trusscot hadn't given up yet; he still had one last card to play.

'Hang on,' he said. 'Surely you haven't forgotten the fly? You saw it yourself – a revolting fly swimming in the soup!'

'That wasn't our fault,' argued Sam.

'No it wasn't,' agreed Mrs Smedley. 'Because you put it there, Mr Trusscot. I saw you scrabbling around under the table. Then you slipped it into my soup along with the salt.'

'MR TRUSSCOT!' cried Mum, shocked.

Dad shook his head.

'Nice try, Trusscot,' he said. 'But you won't win that way.'

Trusscot's face had turned as red as a strawberry tart. He opened his mouth but nothing came out. Looking down, he found three little puppies under a table. If he didn't move they might use him as a lamppost. Mrs Porter came over and swept them up in her arms.

'Oh the little darlings! Aren't they *adorable?*' she cried. 'If only my poor little Pinky were here to see them. Whose are they?'

Sam suddenly remembered his news.

'Actually they're sort of homeless at the moment,' he explained. 'But about Pinky, there's something I wanted to tell you . . .'

Before he could finish, he was interrupted by a woman whose Labrador had been dragging her along the street. The dog sat down outside the cafe and she noticed the sign at the front.

'Are dogs allowed in?' she asked, hopefully.

Sam looked around. Mum was serving Mrs Smedley, while Dad was arguing with Mr Trusscot.

'Of course,' Sam replied. 'Take a seat. I'll get you a bowl of water – for your dog, I mean.'

No sooner had the woman ordered tea and cake, than two more people passed by with their dogs, an Alsatian and a big St Bernard. Both dogs saw the Labrador and the puppies and decided to join them. The cafe was filling up and Sam had to fetch more bowls of water. It reminded him of something Oscar had said about dad being wrong that cafes and dogs don't mix. At the time it had made no sense. He went to the blackboard and wrote something on the sign.

'What on earth are you doing?' asked Dad.

Sam shrugged. 'You said we needed more customers.'

'Yes but I didn't mean dogs,' said Dad. 'They'll have to go.'

'But they're bringing in customers ,' argued Sam. 'Look at all these people!'

He almost said Oscar had been right all along but luckily Trusscot interrupted.

'What the blazes do you call this?' he yelled. 'The place is full of dogs! DOGS!'

'You don't have to shout,' said Sam. 'They're all quite happy.'

'But you can't have DOGS in a cafe!' complained Trusscot. 'It's not allowed!'

'Who says so?' asked Mum, passing with a tray of brownies.

'Yes,' said Sam. 'It's our cafe and we welcome everyone.' He pointed to the sign outside.

DOGS WELCOME!

Free bowl of water for every customer!

'But . . . but this is outrageous!' cried Mr Trusscot. 'And it's against the law. Tell them, Mrs Smedley.'

The health inspector put down her coffee.

'Actually it's not,' she said. 'As long as the dogs keep out of the kitchen, then it's up to the owner who's allowed in.'

Sam and Mum looked at Dad who shrugged and headed back inside. Things were looking up, thought Sam. But he still hadn't had a chance to tell Mrs Porter about Pinky. As it turned out he didn't need to because

Louie arrived on his bike. With him came Oscar leading a pack of thirty or more hungry dogs.

They swarmed into the cafe like an invading army.

Everywhere Sam looked, terriers, pugs, poodles and scruffy mongrels lay on the floor or scooted under tables. They lapped from bowls of water and crunched on pieces of flapjack. Among the crowd a small Pekinese bounded up to

Mrs Porter.

'PINKY! You came back!' she cried, hugging him joyfully. 'Where have you been, you naughty boy?'

Mum and Dad looked around dumbfounded. You couldn't move for dogs. Even Sam had to admit things were getting out of hand.

'Where did they all come from?' shouted Mum, above the noise.

'Oscar brought them,' replied Sam. 'That's what I wanted to tell you. We found them all at a yard where they kept them in filthy cages.'

Oscar suddenly ran out onto the street. Sam caught sight of a vehicle turning the corner at speed. It was the black K9 van and it was coming their way.

Chapter 10

A Grand Day for a Run

Sam ran out and crouched beside Oscar.

'They've come to take them back,' said Oscar. 'We have to put a stop to this.'

'How?' asked Sam.

'Tell the truth,' replied Oscar. 'Why do you think they took Pinky?'

'I don't know, it was a mistake, I suppose,' said Sam.

The driver of the van had spotted them and was slowing down.

Oscar looked at Sam. 'No mistake,' he said. 'Look at these dogs, do they all look like strays to you?'

Sam stared and wondered why he'd never noticed it before. Not only did many of the dogs look well fed, they also had collars. That meant that they probably had owners like Pinky. And if that was true . . .

'Crumble!' gasped Sam.

'Exactly,' agreed Oscar. 'Get ready, here they come.'

The van pulled up outside the cafe and the two uniformed wardens jumped out. For a moment they stood gawping at the cafe thronged with dogs of every kind. Then Carla clenched her fists and marched in.

'Everyone stay calm,' she cried. 'These dogs have escaped and we're here to take them back.'

Oscar stepped forward and growled,

blocking their way.

'It's him, Carla. It's that doolally dog again,' said Harry. 'Look, he's still got white stuff on his fur.'

'Leave him to me,' said Carla, grimly.

She made a grab for Oscar but Sam got in the way.

'You leave him alone, he's my dog!' he cried, bravely.

'And mine!' said Louie. 'Well okay, not mine but he's my friend's.'

Sam's Mum and Dad came over to join them.

'This is our cafe,' said Dad. 'So perhaps you should explain what you're doing here.'

The two wardens hesitated, suddenly aware that they had an audience.

Sam spoke up. 'Mrs Porter, ask them why they stole Pinky,' he said.

'Is that true? Well? I'd like an explanation,' said Mrs Porter.

'We never touched im,' lied Harry.

Mr Trusscot had heard enough. 'This is ridiculous!' he said. 'The Council employs these wardens to pick up strays. It's utter nonsense to claim they've been stealing people's dogs!'

'Is it?' said Sam. 'Then why have lots of them got collars?'

Mum's hand rested on his shoulder. 'Pedigree dogs like Pinky would fetch a lot of money, I imagine,' she said. 'But I suppose you two don't know anything about that?'

Carla swallowed hard. This wasn't working out how they'd planned.

'It's okay, we don't want to cause trouble,' she said. 'Start the van, Harry.'

'Come again? ' said Harry.

'I said, start the van, you dozy nurk!' hissed Carla.

They turned around but Oscar was way ahead of them. A set of keys dangled from his

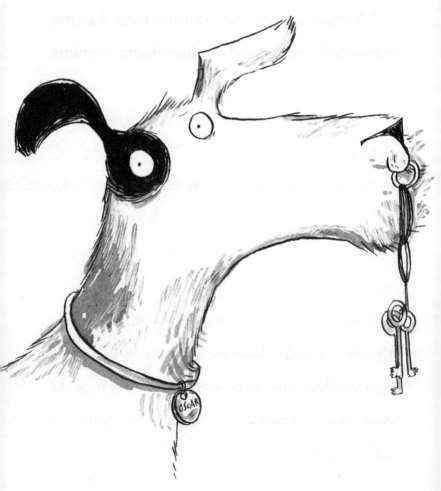

mouth – keys he'd just taken from the van. Carla bit her lip. There were a lot of dogs and suddenly none of them looked too friendly.

'RUN FOR IT, HARRY!' she cried.

The two wardens ran for their lives, barging through the crowd and sending chairs tumbling as they made for the beach.

'Don't let them get away!' cried Dad.

Oscar was the first to set off in pursuit. All dogs love a chase and he was soon joined by Bingo, along with the St Bernard, the Alsatian and an assortment of pugs, mongrels and yapping poodles. Even Pinky joined the chase, not wanting to be left out. They all tore along the beach as if it was a greyhound track. The two wardens had a head start but they could only count on two legs where the chasing pack all had four.

'They're coming, Carla! They're after us!' gasped Harry.

'Don't talk, RUN, you fool!' panted Carla.

Sam and Louie ran down to the beach to get a better view. The chase had crossed the pebbles and reached the wet sand where the going was easier. A few hundred metres ahead Sam could see a wooden breakwater running down to the sea. If the two wardens reached it, they could haul themselves to safety, leaving the dogs stranded below. Harry was flagging though, running like a man who was much better at sitting down. His uniform trousers kept sliding south, so that he had to hold onto them with one hand.

Oscar meanwhile could run all day and his friends showed no signs of tiring. Sam could see they were gaining fast, closing the gap to a few metres. The dognappers saw it too. In desperation, Carla picked up a stick and threw it.

'FETCH!' she shouted.

It was a nice try but it didn't work. There was only one way to escape. The two panting wardens plunged into the icy cold sea, splashing in up to their waists.

'I can't swim, Carla!' wailed Harry.

'Don't worry, dogs hate water!' said Carla.

This turned out to be another thing they were wrong about. The dogs bounded into the water and soon had Harry and Carla surrounded. A ragged half circle stood in the shallows. cutting them off from the land.

Sam saw Oscar step forward out of the pack. He couldn't hear exactly what was said but he thought he could guess. Oscar would be warning the two astonished thieves that if they *ever* tried anything like this again, they'd be very, very sorry.

Somewhere across town a police car siren was wailing.

CHAPTER 11

DOG'S DINNER

A week later, Sam sat outside at the beach cafe with Mum and Louie, enjoying breakfast. Oscar lay by his feet. Dad had rewarded him with his own blue bowl which had *OSCAR* written on it. As usual the cafe was busy with customers, although the name over the door had changed. Now it was called *THE WAGGY DOG CAFE* (Sam's brilliant idea). Dad had needed a bit of convincing – but now he proudly told customers that they ran the only dog-friendly cafe in Little Bunting (which was certainly true). Naturally he'd insisted on a few house rules that were written up on a notice:

No barking,

no biting,

no fighting . . .

(And NO CATS!)

Sam and Oscar had devised a special menu for dogs which offered a choice of the *Bow-Wow Burger* or *Chicken Liver Surprise*. All dogs received a free bowl of water on arrival. The cafe had quickly become a favourite with all the dog owners in town who stopped in for coffee or breakfast. Families had started to drop in too because children loved having dogs to pat, cuddle and stroke.

'This is great,' said Louie. 'We should come here every Saturday.'

'We certainly seem to be doing well,' agreed Mum. 'Who'd ever have thought a dog cafe would be so popular?'

'Oscar, for one,' said Sam.

'Oh yes, Oscar's a lot cleverer than you think,' said Louie with a smile.

Sam glanced at him. He still wasn't sure if his friend suspected Oscar's secret. He'd certainly been keeping a close eye on him. Sam looked up as another customer arrived.

'Hi, Mrs Porter!' he said. 'How are the puppies?'

'Oh they're doing just fine!' laughed Mrs Porter. 'They wake me up every morning by jumping on my bed.'

The puppies lapped from a bowl of water while their proud parents looked on. Mrs Porter had adopted Bingo and Mitzi while Pinky had become the puppies' favourite uncle. Oscar was delighted for his friends and claimed that every home should have six dogs at least.

Only one person wasn't happy with the way things had turned out and that was Mr Truscott. The Councillor had looked pretty foolish when it became known he'd been employing a gang of criminals. He was forced to find a new dogs' home where all the strays could be looked after properly. The Waggy Dog Cafe ran a *Give a Dog a Home* programme with a noticeboard and snapshots of all the dogs.

'Isn't that Mr Trusscot?' asked Sam, as a man hurried past on the other side of the road.

'So it is,' said Mum. 'I think your Dad was keen to have a word with him. MR TRUSSCOT!'

The Councillor was reluctantly persuaded to join them.

'I was beginning to think you were avoiding us, Mr Trusscot,' said Dad, coming out.

'Not at all,' said Trusscot, stiffly. 'I just

happen to think that a dog cafe is ridiculous. Dogs belong outdoors.'

'Well, they *are* outdoors,' Sam pointed out.

'And most people who come say they like having dogs around,' added Dad.

'Well, obviously I am not *most* people,' said Mr Trusscot. 'Now I am rather busy, so I'm afraid I can't stop.'

'But it's Saturday, Mr Trusscot,' Sam reminded him.

'I am well aware what day it is, thank you,' said Trusscot.

'That means we've been open exactly one week today,' said Dad. 'You bet me that the cafe wouldn't last that long.'

'Oh, um, did I?' said Trusscot.

'YES, YOU DID!' said Sam and Mum together.

Trusscot shifted uncomfortably in his seat.

'Very well, I admit it, you won the bet,' he said. 'What do I owe you? Twenty pounds? Fifty?'

He pulled out his wallet but Sam shook his head.

'It wasn't about money,' he said. 'You remember, the loser has to eat a bowl of dog food.'

'And a bet's a bet,' added Louie.

'Certainly, a bet's a bet,' agreed Dad.

Mr Trusscot's face wore a look of horror. 'You can't be serious,' he stammered. 'Surely it was just a joke? Anyway, I don't have any dog food.'

Oscar disappeared inside and returned a moment later with a bowl in his mouth. It contained doggy chunks in a thick gloopy gravy. He set it down beside Sam who placed it on the table.

Trusscot stared at bowl and back at them. He could see they weren't going to let him off the hook. He prodded the soggy brown lumps with a fork and shuddered.

'All of it, every mouthful,' Dad reminded him.

Trusscot speared a chunk of meat, lifted it to his nose and sniffed. He turned a sickly green and his hand flew to his mouth.

'I'm sorry . . .' he croaked and fled from the table.

'It's funny,' said Sam. 'But most dogs seem to like it.'

Oscar's eyes met his. Sam could almost have sworn that he was laughing.

Look out for Oscar and Sam's next extraordinary adventure . . .

OSCAR

AND THE

CATASTROPHE

EGMONT